# POETRY
## OF
# AL BECHERER

Albert Becherer

Copyright © 2017 Albert Becherer
All rights reserved
First Edition

PAGE PUBLISHING, INC.
New York, NY

First originally published by Page Publishing, Inc. 2017

ISBN 978-1-64027-661-1 (Paperback)
ISBN 978-1-64027-662-8 (Digital)

Printed in the United States of America

# PETS

I'm sitting here with the family cat
Thinking about this and that

She sleeps and plays throughout the day
While I'm at work to earn some pay

Maybe at some future time
I'll be the pet, and she'll write rhyme

# LABS

Here's a toast to the loyal lab
They love you even if you are a crab

They really become a part of you
And give you love without a clue

They have the patience of a saint
When they're bad, you'll say they ain't

They find a way into your heart
Sometimes tear the house apart

# MS. LENA

Sitting in my room alone
Very quiet like a stone

Thinking about this and that
Mostly of Ms. Lena my late cat

She was a beauty, solid black
Personality, she did not lack

It really hurt to let her go
But such is life, its ebb and flow

# FEELING

I stand out here for so long
With my thoughts, right or wrong

It's not the place I want to be
It hurts so much I need to flee

I know there's beauty in sight and sound
And hope for my emotions to be found

It's been so long not to feel
I'm looking for a way to heal

To try and change after all these years
Brings me often to the edge of tears

Someday this will all be past
Even as I breathe my last

# DAYLIGHT SAVING TIME

The sun is rising later now since
Man has changed the time
That man can play and with space-time has brought me to this rhyme
If we can change the hours of days
Strictly on a whim
Will all things be perverted and
Nothing left to him

# HUMANS

We humans are a different lot
Who think and reason and feel

We believe and worship a higher being
And then proceed to steal

We rape and maim and sometimes murder
When convicted only ask, "Where can I appeal?"

Maybe someday our race will grow
And our world a chance to heal

# DREAMS

A dreams is but a visual thought
It can be seen but never caught

They come and go on a whim
Sometimes happy sometimes grim

They tell a story at times true
Others will make a fool of you

When you arise from your cot
Some are remembered, but most forgot

# TURKEY SHOPPING

Doing the Thanksgiving shopping I
Thought it would do no harm

To buy a fresh turkey from the
Sam and Ella farm

Left the house early just to beat
The rush

Not knowing that Sam is quite
The drinking lush

He arises daily at twelve or one
or two

Has an eye-opener which heads to
Quite a few

Ella says to pick a bird, they're
All running free

Naturally I found mine perched
high up in a tree

Next year I'll get my turkey
At the local mart

I'll pluck it from the freezer
And put it in my cart

# THERE WAS A TIME

There was a time when life was fine
The world was happy and all mine

There was a time when things were bad
I think of the things I never had

There was a time of fun and play
It was great I must say

There was a time of which I'm not proud
I think of it, but never aloud

There was a time I was in love
But it's gone, flew like a dove

There was a time when I was young and gay
Now I'm old and here to stay

# MOTHER

This poem is for my mother dear
Who has loved me for another year

I know I'm not the perfect child
In fact sometimes I am quite wild

I love you, Mom, and that's for sure
A love so deep, there is no cure

So here's to you, my super mother
You stand alone like no other

# FATE

When a man finally meets his fate
Be it terrible or really great

He knows the things that have been done
He knows if they were mean, or just in fun

He has to pay the piper's price
Be he evil or really nice

Wherever you go or what you do
There's a spirit looking over you

Take a piece of my advice
Cause no trouble, just be nice

# 5 WORDS

A popular saying from my youth
Still applies, it is a truth

Different strokes for different folks
was murmured in between the tokes

It's all accepting in itself
Be you a giant or an elf

You can dwell on it for some time
Five true words that fit in this rhyme

# RHYMES

The poetry I've read of late
Does not contain a rhyme

It does not have a meter
I think it is a crime

This is truly doggerel
A waste of readers' time

It should only be read aloud
By a most insensitive mime

# A POEM

A poem should rhyme, as everyone knows
Otherwise it's simply plain old prose

It's just a newspaper or book of tales
But in my mind, it really fails

These other writings have their place
But they lack the style and grace

So, poets, please rhyme your words
Or else your pap is for the birds.

# WILLIES BUS

I've heard some tales about Willie's bus
Don't understand what is the fuss

If a man wants to have a casual smoke
he'll roll his own and have a toke

I know the law says you can't do that
Who's going to tell, only a rat

A man's business is really his own
Particularly when you're seventy and fully grown

# WRITING

As it often has been said
To be or not is from a poet dead

To bring new reasons to be read
A person must flush and refill his head

The poet's words must ebb and flow
Balance the meter and vocabulary grow

It's not so easy as we all know
That's why when it works, we really crow

# DRUGS

The city's full of coke and crack
The country filled with meth

If we don't get our freedom back
The future is only death

Don't look for all the things we lack
Just take a long deep breath

We're got to do it, both white and black
And follow the drug-free path

# MY PAST

At times I'm truly aghast
When thinking of my checkered past

The things I've done and seen really do amaze
Although some are seen through a purple haze

At times I'm so very good, and others oh so bad
To see the new day made me very glad

I'm starting a new tomorrow with very good intent
I've paid my dues, and now it's to open up and vent

There's so much that I want to do, yet I don't know what
I hope I don't mess it up and fall upon my butt.

But life has always come my way
And led me through the fiery fray

# GARDEN

I like to putter in my yard
nothing difficult or too hard

To raise a tomato or pepper plant
Brings rewards that money can't

When you eat what's raised by your own hand
The meals become truly grand

So if you have some time to waste
grow a garden, but do it posthaste

# LEAVING

It's time for you to leave this place

It's time to say adieu

I'll really miss your friendly face

There's so much to miss about you

You have a special style and grace

I know you'll get your due

# RELAXING

I like to have some time to think

To just pull back from the brink

Just relax and pass the day
In my head it's the only way

I need a place to write my stuff
I don't get there quite enough

And when I write another poem
my inner self says welcome home

# ANOTHER YEAR

Another year has come and gone
Something not to dwell upon

Time moves faster as it fades by
Like a bolt of lightning in the sky

We just go on and pay it no mind
or we will simply stay behind

Happy birthday, I say to you
Take and enjoy, it is your due

# WHAT A DAY

What a day, what a day
The sky has been so grim and grey

What a day, what a day
The boss lets out his normal bray

What a night, what a night
I lock my doors very tight

What a night, what a night
I lie here in total fright
What a morning, what a morning
It's great to see a new day forming,
What a morning, what a morning
The sun is up and brightly burning

# LIFE

Life is not always smiles, sugar, and cream
Sometimes it seems like a very bad dream
I get so angry, I really want to scream
But then I remember my family, my special team
Now I'm returning to life's glowing beam
And flow forever in the unending stream

# PERSPECTIVES

When facing south, the world spins left
Looking north, it's to the right

Both sides in any war can see
only their own light

I'm not a saint or bigot, just
an ordinary man

But if I can see this problem
Anybody can

To resolve any problem, walk in
Another's shoes

If you don't believe me, watch the
Evening news

We come into this world free of cares
or fear or hates

We're taught that we are different
And everybody rates

We've got to change the system of
Teaching right and wrong

Or this world as we know, it won't
be here very long

# RETIREMENT

I'm going to retire and live the life of ease
The only major problem, I won't know who to please

I've always had a boss to tell me of the goal
Now it will be only me and my fishing pole

I worked hard to get where I'm at
And now I'll have the responsibility of my cat

I'm going to do the things I like, give it my best shot
But I'll probably wind up in the same old pot

This is very scary yet exciting, my dear friend
It's another beginning, not the very end.

# DIRECTIONS

East is east and west is west
The two shall never meet

I sit here in the great Midwest
Oh, what a lovely seat

The East Coast sees the sunrise first
That's a special treat

The West Coast sees the sunset last
They think it's very neat
I'll stay here in the middle
With the corn and wheat

# Y2K

After all the hoopla about Y2K
I have only this to say

It's P. T. Barnum at his best
Won't the media give it a rest

There's nothing at all to fear
It's just another brand new year

The talking heads and their ilk
Will find someone else to bilk

The public is treated as pawn
The news today makes me want to yawn

Get away from the sensational hype
Forget the rumors and useless tripe

Let's hear the news, both good and bad
Let us decide what makes us mad

# THANKSGIVING

Thanksgiving is a special day
In our country the USA

Anticipation puts us in the mood
Then fills us up with good food

We must remember to give thanks
For those who gave in the ranks

There is so much of everything
It makes everyone want to sing

So gather around and fill your plate
And all your wants we will sate

For this is one special day
Stuff yourself, you really may

# THE EARTH

A place of storms and clouds and rain
from this the earth is made

A place of war of hate and death
Of this we're all dismayed

A place of loving and giving and sharing
of this we're all apart

A place of beauty and fire and ice
from where we got our start

A place of trees, of cactus, and crops
for which we share the air

A place of serpent, of fish and fowl
for which we are to care

# SPECIAL RIDE

I'd like to ride a lightning bolt
flashing through the sky

To speed along in space in the
Twinkling of an eye

I'd like to see all the stars
In the Milky Way

To visit other planets just to
Pass the day

I'd like to do some different things
While I'm here on earth

To laugh and learn and love and live
Just for what it's worth

# SIRENS

I heard a siren far off in the night

I hope everyone is all right

It could be fine, it could be a wreck

Or maybe a speeder trying to break
his neck

# BIRDS

Two birds sitting on a wire
One says "We can't get much higher"

Other says "I really don't know"
Why…Don't we just go go go

First bird says I'm getting sick
I best dive down real quick

Second one says not so fast
I really want this *high* to last

# OBESE

Home again, home again jiggity jig
Needing to change, still fat as a pig

Huffing and puffing, can't blow the house down
Needing to diet, resolutions abound

Like Little Miss Muffet eating curds and whey
Maybe I'll change and get thin someday

It's like finding the golden egg goose
Get your ducks in a row and turn your
Mind loose

# MIDNIGHT RAINBOW

I'm looking for a midnight rainbow
far off in the night

It's big and bold and very rare. A
truly beautiful sight

I do not know the hues and shades
in the darkened sky

The only thing that's constant is
my search upon the high

I want to find my quarry and show
It to the world

To prove that moonlight is magic and
Old ideas can be twirled

This is not an easy task of this I'm
Very sure

It is not the job that draws me
It's such a lovely lure

# MONSTER

There's a monster under my bed
With razor teeth and eyes so red

He has many needs to be fed
But they're not, meat, or pasta, or bread

His appetite fills me with dread
I thank goodness he's all in my head

# GAMES

Remember when we played our games
We learned to keep our eye on the *ball*

Our live are forever changing we need
To stand straight and *tall*

We play a game, it's called life, the
Prize is *all*

We must fight and scream and as always
Keep our eye on the ball

We and our friends and neighbors need
To answer the call

We gave our time, our blood, our limbs
We gave our lives, but kept our eye on the ball

# BOUNCING BALL

Life is like a bouncing ball going up
And down

You have a lot of smiles, occasionally
A frown

Paying for the changes, trying to find
What's due

Doing what is needed, giving a
Follow-through

It's not so easy to stay on top
The ball, it has a spin

You have to handle all the twists and
Turns if you want to win

# A WAKE

I went to a friend's wake today
his passing was sudden, don't know what to say

He is saluted by all his friends and kin
He wasn't perfect, he had more than one sin

We all reminisced, worried, and fretted
We talked of the past, which some regretted

Most in attendance are at the age
When could be next upon the stage

But don't be unhappy, don't you cry
We'll all meet again up in the sky

# THUGS

Underneath the streetlight bright
I came upon an awful sight
Two gangs of boys ready to fight
Trying to prove might is right

If they were shown some family skills
And had a job that paid the bills
Maybe the mountains would be more like hills
And life would have much different thrills

# LIFE

Life is full of tears and joy
for every single girl and boy
every day is a shiny new toy
Like the horse they found at Troy

It looks good without a doubt
But leads to such an awful rout
No matter what your peers may tout
Be your own person, not a simple lout

# LOOKING

It's so easy from the outside
Looking down or looking in

To talk about others
At a place you've never been

Life has its ups and downs
Take it with a grin

Choices need to be made
Just try not to sin

So live your life as best you can
Don't get caught up in the din

# YESTERDAY

Yesterday is but a thought
Tomorrow is just a dream

Last month is an eternity
Next week is full of steam

Time is ever marching on
As quickly as a stream

You cannot stop or hold it
We can only shine it, really make it gleam

It will look good in history
If we can hide the ugly seam

# BEST POEM

I dream of writing the world's best poem
with perfect pitch and meter

In any language it would rhyme
With thoughts to make someone a leader

And quell the evil thoughts and deeds
of every wife- and child-beater

# DIVORCE

I heard the judge's words again
You're released from marital pain

Answer only to yourself
Put responsibility on the shelf

The freedom to be on your own
Not listening to some crone

Spend time as you wish
Stay at home, or just go fish

# ME

Looking at my checkered past
Wondering why my marriages don't last

Maybe it's a gene I lack
Many mistakes I can't keep track

Then again, it may not be me
Something in them I did not see

No need to worry about that anymore
I'm through with weddings, that's for sure

# MARRIAGE

Thinking about the tie that binds
Or is it just a vow that grinds

The weddings don't always last
Some disappear really fast

At times it's for a new mate
That can lead to a different fate

As it has been said before
Wait, be sure, don't slam the door

# LOVE

I've been in love several times
About which there's been some rhymes

Funny thing none were the same
They were quiet, or loud, or totally insane

Each was special in its way
I found love is not child's play

Now I'm an older and wiser man
No more women in my plan

# WIVES

I've had three wives, that's a lot
If women were booze, I'd be a sot

My life has been mixed and muddled
I just want to be pampered and cuddled

When thinking about what could have been
That's what is the real sin

But nothing ventured, nothing gained
My mind is blank, but my memory stained

# ADIEU

Our relationship is over, time to say adieu
We had some good times, just me and you

The high point was a kitchen embrace
It was only a moment, left no trace

At times we both did our worst
Emotions exploded, tempers burst

I have only one thing to say
You don't throw thirty-six years away

# IRAQ II

Alex is going to play in the sand
once more

Going to a place we all abhor

Wish him luck and offer a prayer

That he'll be safe over there

There's historic places to go and see

Courtesy of Uncle Sam and the USMC

Play it safe but have some fun

See the world over the barrel of a gun

Keep your thoughts open, your mind on track

Do what needs to be done and hurry
Back

# LOVE YOU

I love you for the things you are

I love you for the things you're not

I'll love you for a million years

I'll love you 'til I rot

I love you in both thick and thin

I love you no matter what we got

I love you like the spring loves green

I just thought of something, I love you
A lot

# A DATE

I've wracked my brain and thought
And thought, wondering what to do

To try and bring us closer, A
Bond for me and you

I think we should plan a special
Date, not a quickie dinner

And then I have another thing
I've got to get much thinner

I think that in the planning, we
Will talk much more

It might put some life in us, not
Be another chore

This really means a lot to me, It
Is my future life

I want to make the most of it,
With you, my lovely wife

# CHRISTMAS

Christmas is the time to give
Money passes, like water through a sieve

The weather is cold, often snowy
houses lit, very showy

My gift is all my love, heart, and soul
It goes so deep, it's an unfillable hole

These words don't seem like quite enough
But in my mind, it beats the other stuff

# VALENTINE'S DAY

This is the day to show our love
To say we really care

A time to thank the stars above
If we only dare

If we fit like hand in glove
Do our very best to share

Our future will be like the dove
Peaceful in our lair

# SPEND SOME TIME

I want to spend some time with you
To see what our special love can do

Tell you what, I'll spend the night
In the morning we'll be all right

We'll take our time and cruise along
Making our music, creating a song

We can have a wonderful life
If you will agree to be my lovely wife

# TIME FLIES

Say good-bye to tomorrow, it's already
Yesterday

Isn't it amazing how time can slip away

It seems we only met a little while ago

But here we are together, heads as white
As snow

Looking forward to our future, we'll have
Another life

We'll go on forever being man and
Wife

# SHIP OF LOVE

I wrote this poem of love for you
To tell you how I feel

After all that we've be through
Sometimes I've been a heel

One thing I know for sure, my love for you is true
I may not have the zest or maybe not true zeal

My love for you is stronger than any witches' brew
It cannot be denied, no one can repeal

May I can show you in our next life or two
Our love is a feast a never-ending meal

Thinking back about our love, how it grew and grew
We're like a beautiful ship of love, a rudder and
A keel

# DEJA VU

Passing through the world one life

I met my very favorite wife

Did I know her long ago

I've asked and asked, I do not know

But if we meet when the future comes

I hope we act like old alums

# KIDS

Here's to my kids, I do not jest
I hope they know I did my best

I'm far from perfect as we all know
I tried to teach and let you grow

Now that my job is finally done
I see yours has just begun

Please learn from my mistakes and errors
So your kids can be better to theirs

# 30 YEARS

We've been together for thirty-plus years
Shared many smiles, shed a few tears

We don't always agree about this and that
We do share a bed with a very spoiled cat

I love you now as I did back then
Both as a woman and my very best friend

Loving each other is a two-way street
Giving and taking is our special treat

I love you now, I'll love you again
In our next life and then the next ten

# PERFECT MAN

I know I'm not a perfect man
I've chased my tail, just ran and ran

What I do is never enough
I'm told it's nothing, it's all just fluff

Trying to have a talk with you
Must be your way or it just won't do

I listen to your words and nod
Often agree, so as not to be odd

These are not the words you want to hear
This is my way of being clear

Nothing will change you or me
I think, on this, we both agree

You have your way, right or wrong
I have mine, we both feel strong

I don't know what can change these facts
We go over and over, like a play with four acts

# HURTING

The sun's rising once again
Seems like he's my only friend

You did me wrong one more time
It's happened so often, it's a real crime

I toss and turn the whole night through
Trying to rid my thoughts of you

But I'll survive and love once more
Right now I hurt the tears just pour

When I'm done with the tears and dread
Know my true love is up ahead

# LIFE GOES ON

Looking forward and looking back
My life appears completely black

I do my best to help around
Only to get knocked back down

Life goes on, good or bad
I have no clue which I've had

Nothing has a hold on me
No past or future I can see

I'll go on until my end
Hoping still to find a friend

# WASHINGTON DC

Washington DC must be an evil place
Everyone runs at an awful pace

We send our honest and friendly rep.
When they return they're out of step

Most are poor when they go
Then come back home with lots of dough

They promised to build a perfect tower
Come back home full of greed and power

You can't trust the evil left
The right is stealing with much deft

The media has forgotten what's news
Presents to us its slanted views

# CRIME

The crime rate is beyond belief
What's the difference, just another thief

The NSA. The FBI. The Justice Dept. too
Are run slightly better than a forsaken zoo

I do not have an answer, nor have I a plan
I'm just a humble poet, an ordinary man

# POLITICIANS

The politicians are at it again
Bringing on the promise train

They tell you what you want to hear
Or spread lies to create some fear

Most have never had a real job
They only know how to bitch and sob

I think we should start from scratch
Get rid of them all, for a new batch

# VOTING

Tuesday is our time to vote
Know your choices, make a note

We need to get rid of the religious right
Also get out of the Iraqi fight

Taxes need to be clear and fair
Make it a flat tax if you dare

We need a person for our times
A person of quality, free of crimes

We need to unite our country again
Shake hands with an enemy, make him a friend

# WHAT I THINK

This is a quick poem to tell what I think
When facing Washington, I detect a stink

The party lines don't matter, they're all the same
They think only money, their only game

Someday when the lawyers reach their final
Reward
They'll find the right decisions not
Too hard

# CHANGES

Thinking about the forest full of
Life and breath
Winter sends a frigid blast bringing
Cold death

But another season soon beginning, a green
And rainy spring
A start of life for flora and fauna
A wonderful beautiful thing

Then there comes a dryer time, a
Totally different drummer
The days are long and hot, it
Happens every summer

Then there is the other season
Beautiful to all
This is the season that I love, when
Leaves begin to fall

# FREEDOM

Don't be angry, don't be shy
Don't even think about a cry

We've been here before under attack
We've got to go forward, we can't go back

Our freedoms have come long and hard
We must protect them, stay on our guard

There are some people who act like a friend
Keep your eye them buddy, they'll bite your
Rear end

Listen to my warning, listen to my word
Stand and be a person, not a member of the
Herd

# WAR AND OIL

With most of the shooting over
And done
It's easy to think the war has been won

We choose to think our foes are on the
Run
When in reality, the war has just
Begun

The oil men think this is lots of
Fun
They're going to make money by the
Ton

This war will go on as long as there
Is a sun
Unless we come to our senses and
Live as one

# IRAQ I

Here's a note to Alex, playing in the sand
He got himself a free trip to an exotic land

They gave him special clothing, it includes a
Mask
Not much to do all day, but sit in the sun
And bask

I thought about our duck trips in cold and
Wet and damp
And now another uncle has sent you
Off to camp

You're in my thoughts every day and night
If it comes to war remember, "Just do it" right

# SPRING

The woods are coming alive today
The leaves are turning green, hooray

Every spring, nature starts life anew
Even the sky is a richer blue

The birds are chirping and the turkeys call
It'll be this way until the fall
The chimes are ringing in the gentle breeze
Thank God and Joyce Kilmer for making trees

# THE SUN

The sun came up again today
He didn't have much to say

It started a long time ago
How many years, I do not know

It will go on forevermore
Until it burns to its core

# THE SEA

Out upon the shiny sea
A peaceful place for you and me

When you look both fore and aft
You're glad you're on a sturdy craft

Then at night the perfect blend
Sea and sky have no end

When the morning sun comes up
The beauty overflows one's cup

# SUNSET

I watched the sunset today
Looking to see its final ray

It is always a beautiful sight
Fading into the very last light

The same will happen again tomorrow
So if you miss it, have no sorrow

The same but different every day
That is all there is to say

# 4 SEASONS

I love the weather of early spring
So crisp and cool, makes you want to sing

The heat of summer can bring you down
And turn the green to dirty brown

Fall is the return of the cool
In weather terms, a perfect jewel

And then comes winter, clean and white
The end of the year done up right

# SEDONA RED

There is a place to stretch my head

This beautiful place is Sedona Red

The vortices to where we were led

Are all around Sedona Red

It may be called the devil's bed

But take me back to Sedona Red

No matter what else is said

There is only one Sedona Red

# TETONS

To view the Tetons is an awesome sight
Especially on a full moon night

The sunny peaks with lakes below
Are a perfect nature show

Yellowstone is not far away
With Old Faithful on display

Walking through the geyser site
Reminds one of the earth's real might

When you see the waterfall
You truly have heard nature's call

Floating the snake is a fantastic trip
You need a guide so you don't flip

So if nature beauty is what you seek
Northwest Wyoming is up your creek

# SNOW

It snowed upon us again last night
Awaking in the morning, it's a beautiful sight

All white and shiny on the ground
Stuck to the trees all around

Another of nature's beauty points
With a blanket the earth anoints

It gives us vision, hope, and reason
To look forward to another season

# THE YEAR

As I look out at a sky so gray
It's just another winter day

I'm in a hurry for early May
When flowers bloom, and children play

In July, it gets so hot
The garden needs water a lot

October cools, believe it or not
It's time to have a beer and "brat"

# THE MOON

Did you ever watch the moon at night
It's truly an amazing sight

It floats between the clouds so bright
Its color is awesome white

When it's full and shines just right
It lights your ways, eases your fright

But even when it's a sliver so slight
It pushes the tides with all its might

As it makes its nightly flight
I hold my true love very tight

# STREAM

I sit beside a beautiful stream

Watching every glint and gleam

You dare not plot and do not scheme

For this will be tomorrow's dream

# YESTERDAY, TODAY, TOMORROW

Sitting here upon this rock
Time stands still, there is no clock

The water rushing all around
My thoughts are deep, so profound

Today is all there is to life
Tomorrow is maybe, yesterday is strife

Being here is such a thrill
Come back tomorrow, I think I will

# WATERFALL

I hear the cataracts mighty splash
It rushes past in such a flash

A never-ending ear splitting roar
Making one's spirit soar

It's nature's way to make water clean
Ending in a pool quite serene

# RAIN

The afternoon of gentle rain
Spatters on my window pane

It wets the grounds just enough
For the grass, trees, and other stuff

It does appear a little dreary
Waiting for the sun can be leary

Tomorrow will be another change
That's a fact, nothing strange

# NOON

Not many poems written about noon
But many about the sun and the moon

Noon is just a time of day
About which poets have little to say

Noon, I hope to change that fact
With these words I start the act

It can never be too soon
To write about lunchtime, noon

# SUNSET COLORS

Clouds are grey, the edges a pinkish
Hue
Sky beyond is a fantastic sapphire
Blue

Silver stars will soon twinkle
Bright
As we move into the black of
Night

The golden shine of a harvest moon
Means we will have snowy winter soon

Mother Nature has an awesome pallet
You can try, but you'll never match it

# GOLDEN LEAF

While walking in the woods one day
I found a golden leaf

It had a shape and texture that
I had never seen

I looked around both high and low
With some amount grief

To find the source of this rare gift
When it was new and green

Spending time among the trees no
Matter how short and brief

You'll find Mother Nature truly
Is a queen

Someday I'll find that tree that shared
With me its leaf

Then I'll sit upon the ground
Against the trunk I'll lean

# FALL DAY

Beautiful leaves of red and gold
Morning air so crisp and cold

A late fall day in the Midwest
One of Mother Nature's very best

Summer is in the rearview mirror
Winter still has time to appear

The years go by so very fast
I hope that this is not my last

# WINTER DAY

Fresh snow and ice upon the trees
Gently falling in the breeze

Icy covering so clean and white
Gleaming in the sun so bright

The temperature is crisp and cold
Outside is only for the very bold

Stay inside by the cozy warm fire
With the one I love, that's my desire

# CYCLES

The sun shines a golden light
Shows its beam so very bright

They place their blessing on everything
The cycle starts in early spring

Then continues through summer and fall
Providing a rich harvest for us all

The winter starts a hasty retreat
The earth surely sheds its heat

The season starts all over again
Like there is a master plan

# FALLING STAR

While racing with the moon one
Night, I passed a falling star
I asked it where it came from
The answer was afar

It had a silver tail so bright
And all agleam
When I tried to ride it, I
Awakened from my dream

I search the skies both night and
Day, looking for my friend
Hoping we will meet again before
I reach my end

I want the world to see my star
So big and bright and free
Know the reason for this poem
The star is really me

# A SEED

I stand here on the golden shore
Thinking that I need more

Wanting not for food or drink
Having love and the freedom to think

My mind is running fast and wild
Unrestrained, like a very young child

Pondering over this grinding need
Asking for a germ of a seed

I suppose this is what drives me on
To last the night until another dawn

# QUESTIONS

Should I write about the lovely
Sky
Perhaps an ode to the butterfly

It's always tough to make a decision
When your choice can be met with vicious
Derision
Joyce Kilmer said it about the tree
Someday I hope that will be me

To write the words to bring one
fame
The magic blend that is my aim.

# ABOUT THE AUTHOR

Born in 1937, Al Becherer is the oldest of seven children—six boys and one girl. He was raised in St. Louis, Missouri, finished high school, entered the Army first infantry division during peace time, and went to work for a wholesale floor covering company. He retired after forty-two years. He has three ex-wives, one son, and three grandsons.